For Rebecca and Joshua, with all my love – D.G.

For Auntie Barbara, one of the Bangor Night Owls! xx – A.B.

BLOOMSBURY CHILDREN'S BOOKS
Bloomsbury Publishing Plc
50 Bedford Square, London, WC1B 3DP, UK

BLOOMSBURY, BLOOMSBURY CHILDREN'S BOOKS and the Diana logo are trademarks of Bloomsbury Publishing Plc

First published in Great Britain 2020 by Bloomsbury Publishing Plc

A catalogue record for this book is available from the British Library

ISBN 978 1 5266 0349 4 (HB)
ISBN 978 1 5266 0348 7 (PB)
ISBN 978 1 5266 0347 0 (eBook)

2 4 6 8 10 9 7 5 3 1

Printed in China by Leo Paper Products, Heshan, Guangdong

All papers used by Bloomsbury Publishing Plc are natural, recyclable products from
wood grown in well managed forests. The manufacturing processes conform to
the environmental regulations of the country of origin.

To find out more about our authors and books visit www.bloomsbury.com and sign up for our newsletters

Little Owl's Bedtime

Debi Gliori   Alison Brown

BLOOMSBURY
CHILDREN'S BOOKS
LONDON OXFORD NEW YORK NEW DELHI SYDNEY

Little Owl was snuggled up with Mummy Owl
sharing a bedtime story. It was late o'clock.

"Then all the little bunnies closed their eyes and
fell fast asleep. The end," said Mummy.
"Now it's your turn, Little Owl. Close your eyes and . . ."

"NO," said Little Owl.

"No?" said Mummy Owl.

"NO," said Little Owl.
"I don't want to close my eyes. I don't
want to fall asleep. I don't want The End.
I want another story."

Mummy Owl blinked.
"IF I read you one more story," she said,
"promise me you'll snuggle down and go to sleep.
It is VERY late for little owls."
Little Owl nodded.

Mummy Owl read Little Owl another story.

"Then all the little field mice closed their eyes and
fell fast asleep. The end. Goodnight, Little Owl,"
Mummy whispered, "sweet dreams."
"Sweet dreams," said Little Owl.

But . . .

Little Owl's pillow
was **too lumpy**.

Little Owl's quilt
was **too hot**.

Little Owl's eyes
refused to stay shut.

It was very dark.
"Mummy?" Little Owl called.

"Oh, Little Owl," said Mummy Owl.
"It has to be dark so that nobody can see
the very shy frogs when they come out
to sing in the Bashful Frog Chorus."

"I can't hear them," said Little Owl.

"That's probably because they're **very** shy," said Mummy Owl.

"Look, here's a **tiny night light** for you. It's so small even a very shy frog wouldn't mind you using it. Goodnight, Little Owl."

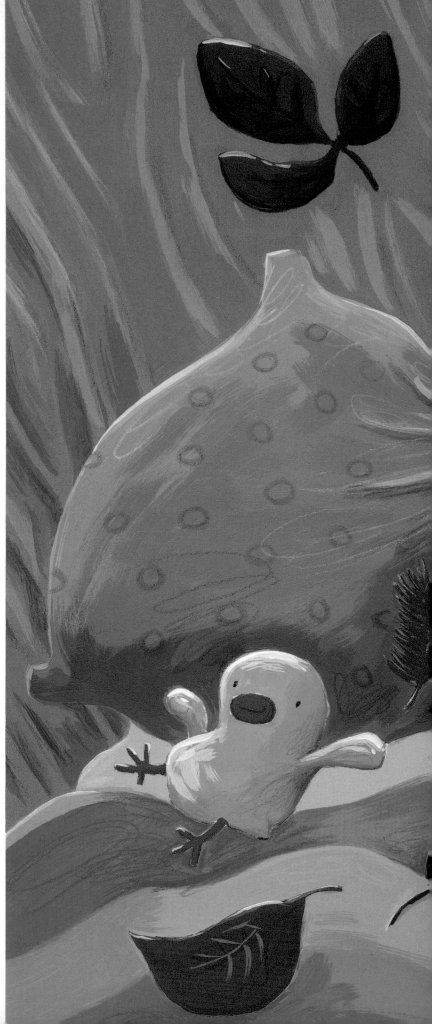

Little Owl closed his eyes.
His pillow was **even lumpier** than before.
Little Owl wriggled and squirmed.

Suddenly Little Owl had an **awful** thought.
"MUMMY!" he called. "I've lost
Hedge and I can't sleep without her!"

"Oh, Little Owl," sighed Mummy.
"Hedge has probably gone to pick up a
midnight snack at the Acorn Bakery."

"Found her!" said Little Owl.
"Look, she was hiding under my pillow."
"Phew!" said Mummy.
"GoodNIGHT, Little Owl."

"And Hedge," said Little Owl.
"Night, night, Hedge," said Mummy Owl.
"Now both of you – Go. To. Sleep."

Hedge fell asleep at once.
Little Owl tried to go to sleep. He tried REALLY hard.
But there was a noise.

"MUMMY!"

"What's that n-n-noise?" squeaked Little Owl.
Mummy listened. "Is that the song of the bashful frogs?"
"No," said Little Owl. "It's a sort of quiet, snorty kind of noise."

"Oh, Little Owl," whispered Mummy Owl,
"I know exactly what that is . . ."

"It's the sound
of **baby butterflies**
snoring in their flowerbeds.
So **sweet.**
We're so lucky to hear them."

"Goodnight, Little Owl,"
said Mummy Owl **again.**

And all was quiet until . . .

"MUMMY!" called Little Owl.

"I'M TOO HOT.

I'M HUNGRY.

I NEED A W. . ."

"Oh, LITTLE OWL,"
said Mummy.

"Look, you've woken up Hedge.
Poor Hedge! Let's tuck her back in."

"Mummy?" said Little Owl.
"Yes, Little Owl," sighed Mummy Owl.
"I can't fall asleep because I'm too
excited about seeing Grandma and
Grandpa Owl tomorrow."

"My dear Little Owl," said Mummy Owl.
"Shall I tell you a secret? Tomorrow will
happen much faster when you fall asleep."
"Really?" yawned Little Owl.
"I promise," said Mummy.

"You forgot to give me a kiss," said Little Owl.
"Silly Mummy," said Mummy Owl. "Love you, Little Owl."
"Love you, too, Mummy," said Little Owl.

Little Owl settled down with Hedge.

"I'll read you one more story, Hedge, but you have
to promise to go to sleep afterwards because
the faster you go to sleep, the faster tomorrow
will come. And tomorrow we're going to see
Grandma Owl and Grandpa Owl."

Little Owl turned off his night light.
"It is dark but I'm right here beside you."
Little Owl tucked Hedge in.

"That sound? It's just Mummy Owl singing in the bath.
Night, night, Hedge, sleep tight."

Little Owl couldn't wait for tomorrow to begin.
He closed his eyes extra tight, pulled the quilt up to his eyes and
snuggled deep into his pillow with a huge, happy yawn.

Mummy Owl tiptoed in for one last kiss.
"Sweet dreams, Little Owl."